A Visit to FAIRYLAND

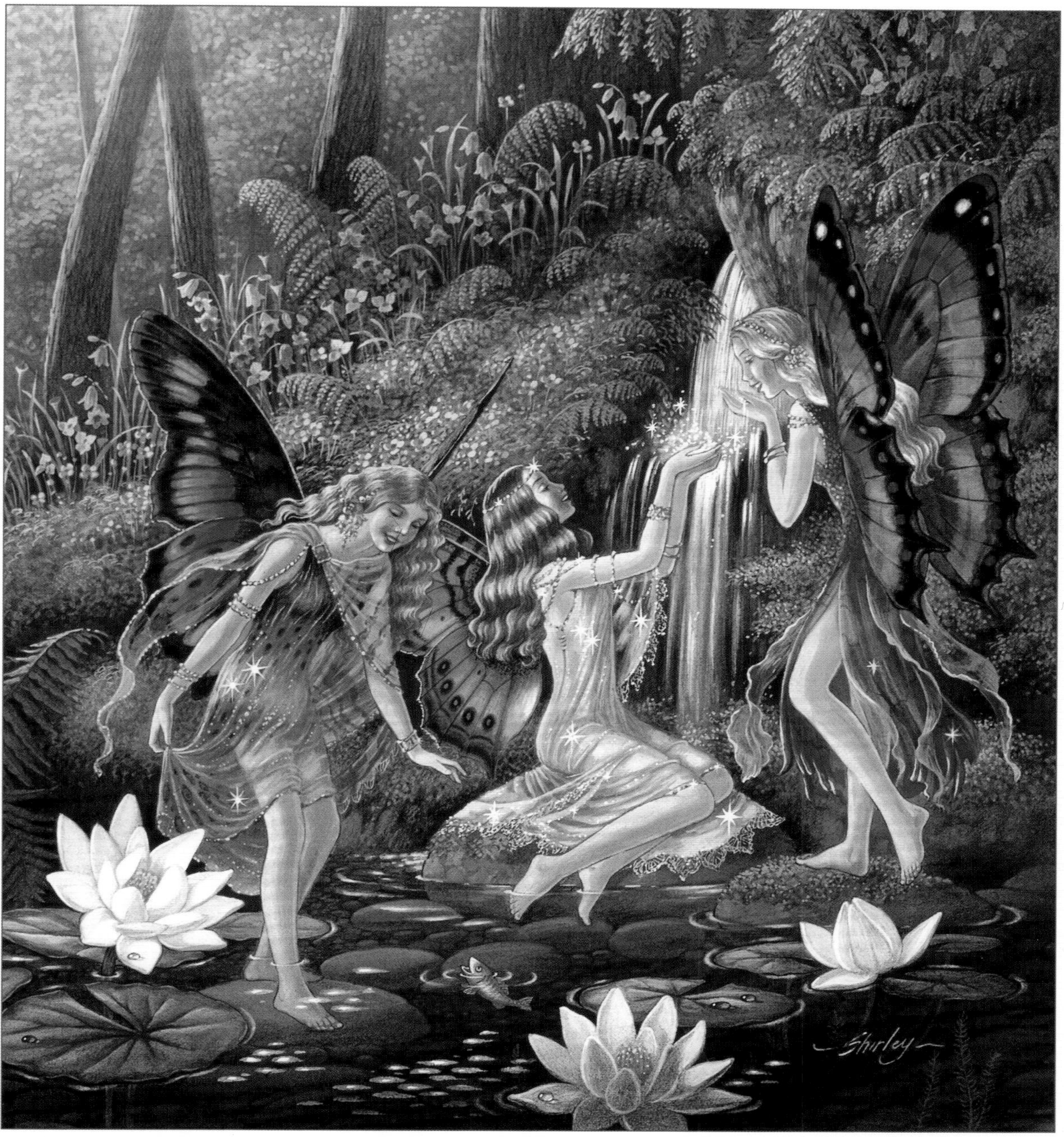
Shirley

by Shirley Barber

PUBLISHED BY BROLLY BOOKS

"There are fairies at the bottom of the garden,"
Laura told her mother.
"In the old willow tree, there is a green door,
and when the fairies open it you can see right into Fairyland!"

"Yes, dear," replied her mother, who was busy cooking.
"Now, why don't you take your little brother into the garden?
You can show him that door to Fairyland!"

Laura knew her mother thought she was just pretending,
and she felt rather hurt. Still, she took her brother
Daniel's hand and led him into the garden.

"Shh, Danny," she whispered, when they
reached the willow tree.
"If we are very quiet, the fairies might come out to talk to us."

Sure enough, after a few minutes the green door opened. . .
and out came the fairies.

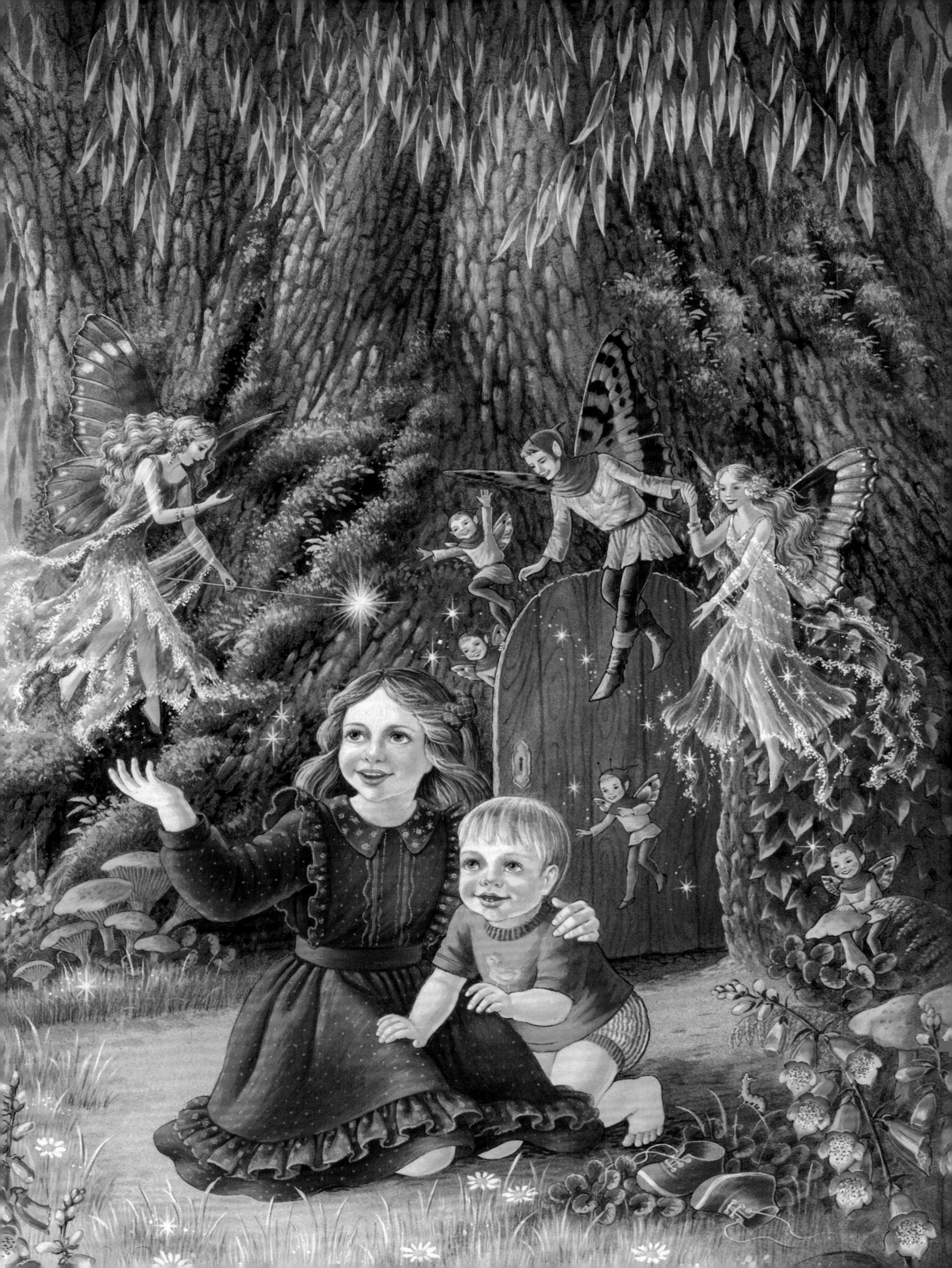

"Would you like to come through this little doorway and see Fairyland?" asked the fairies.

"Oh, yes!" exclaimed Laura. Then she and Daniel crawled through the doorway and found themselves in Fairyland.

Before them was a toadstool town where pixies and other fairy folk were busy shopping and chatting, just like people. Daniel trotted off to explore the narrow twisting streets.

"Don't go too far, you might get lost," warned his sister. "Stay close so I can keep an eye on you!"

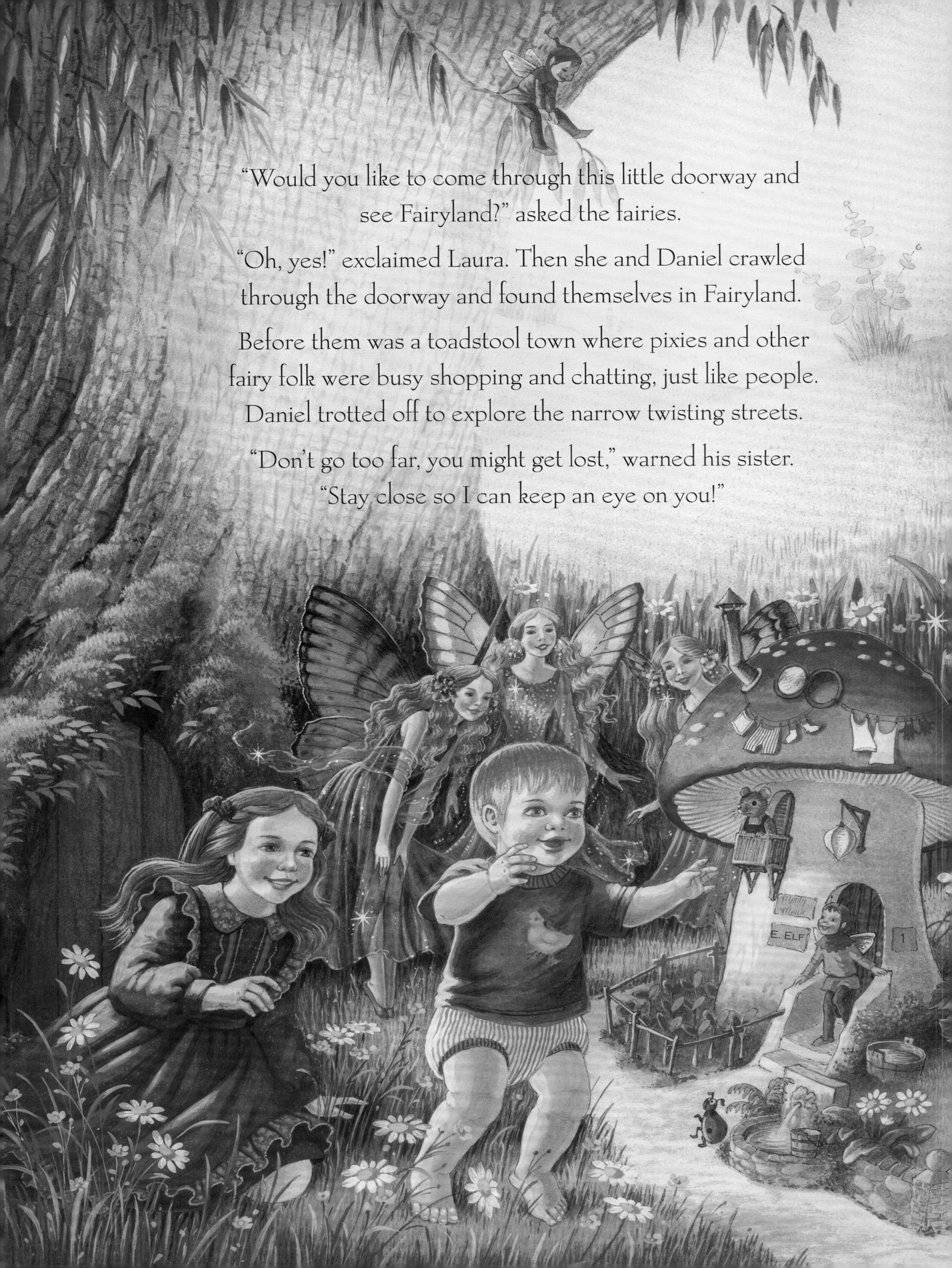
Monty Mouse
E. ELF
1

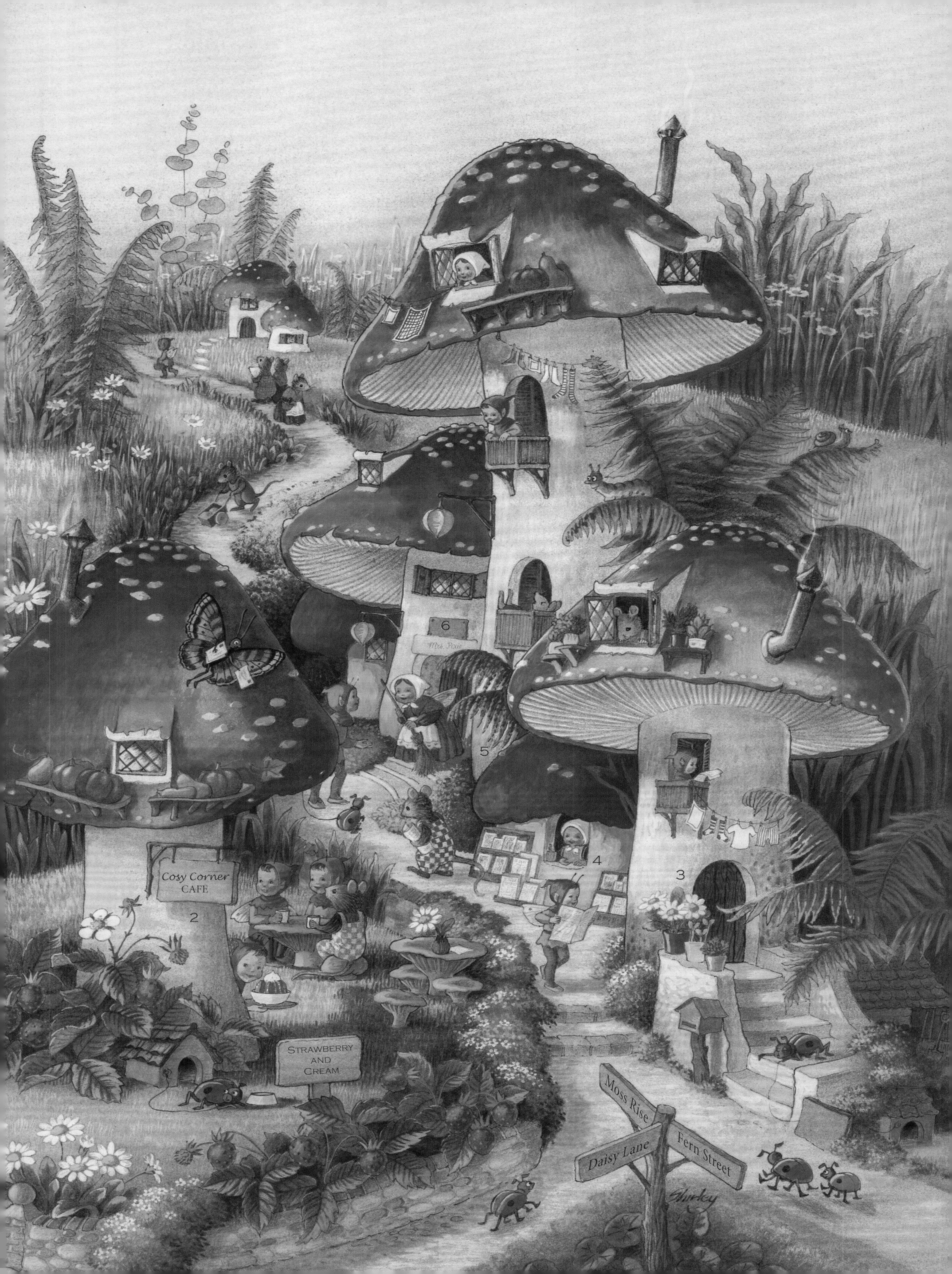
6
Mrs Pixie
5
4
3
Cosy Corner
CAFE
2
STRAWBERRY
AND
CREAM
Moss Rise
Daisy Lane
Fern Street
Shirley

To Daniel the toadstool houses were just like a toy village and he wanted to play with the pixies.

Laura watched him running about for a while, then she noticed further away a garden full of big flowers.

"Come along, Danny," she coaxed. "Let's go and look at those beautiful flowers."

The flowers were so large that Daniel soon forgot the toadstool houses and ran to look at them. Inside each flower a fairy baby was curled up as if in its cradle.

"This is where our babies live till they are old enough to fly," a fairy nurse told the children.

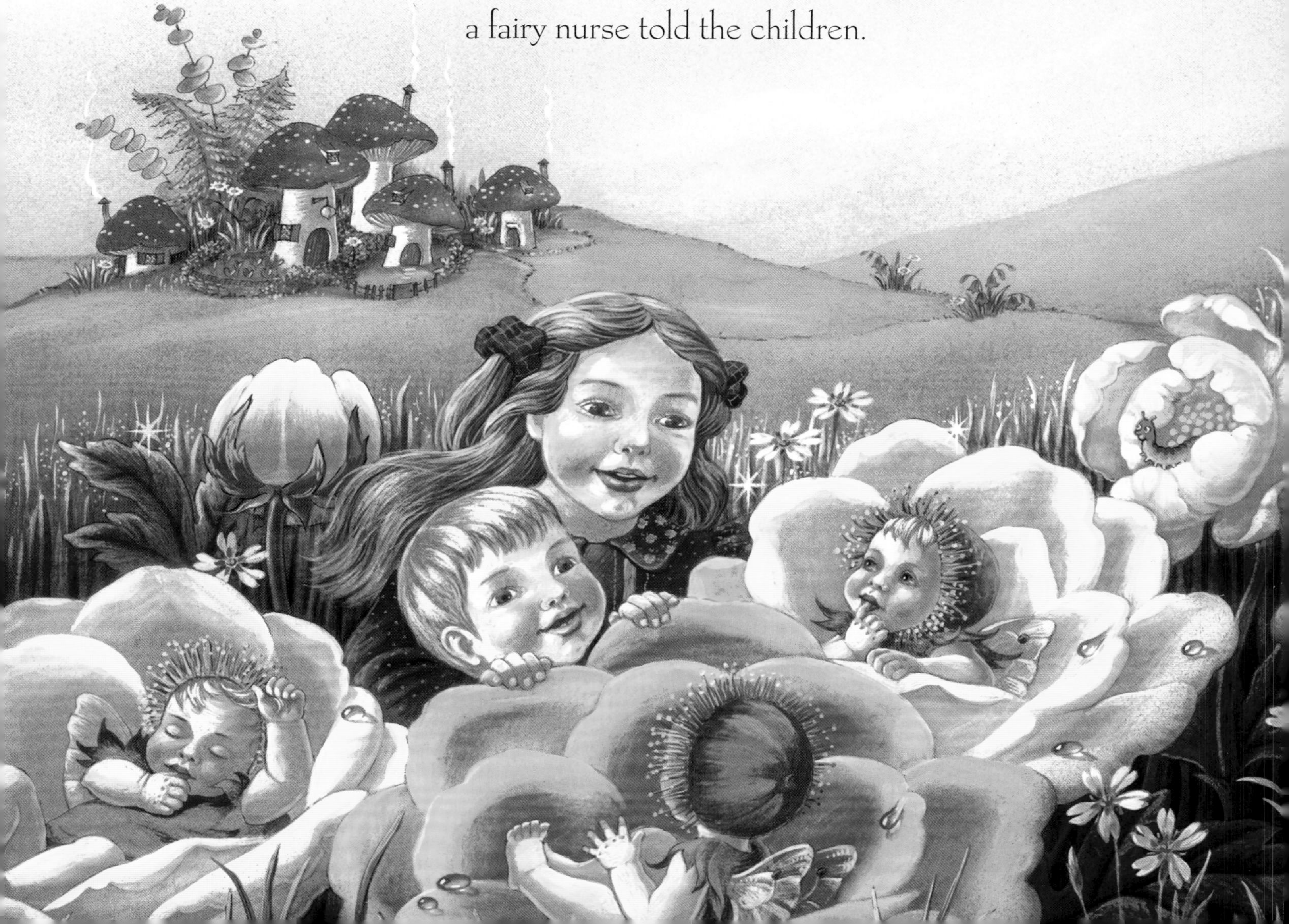

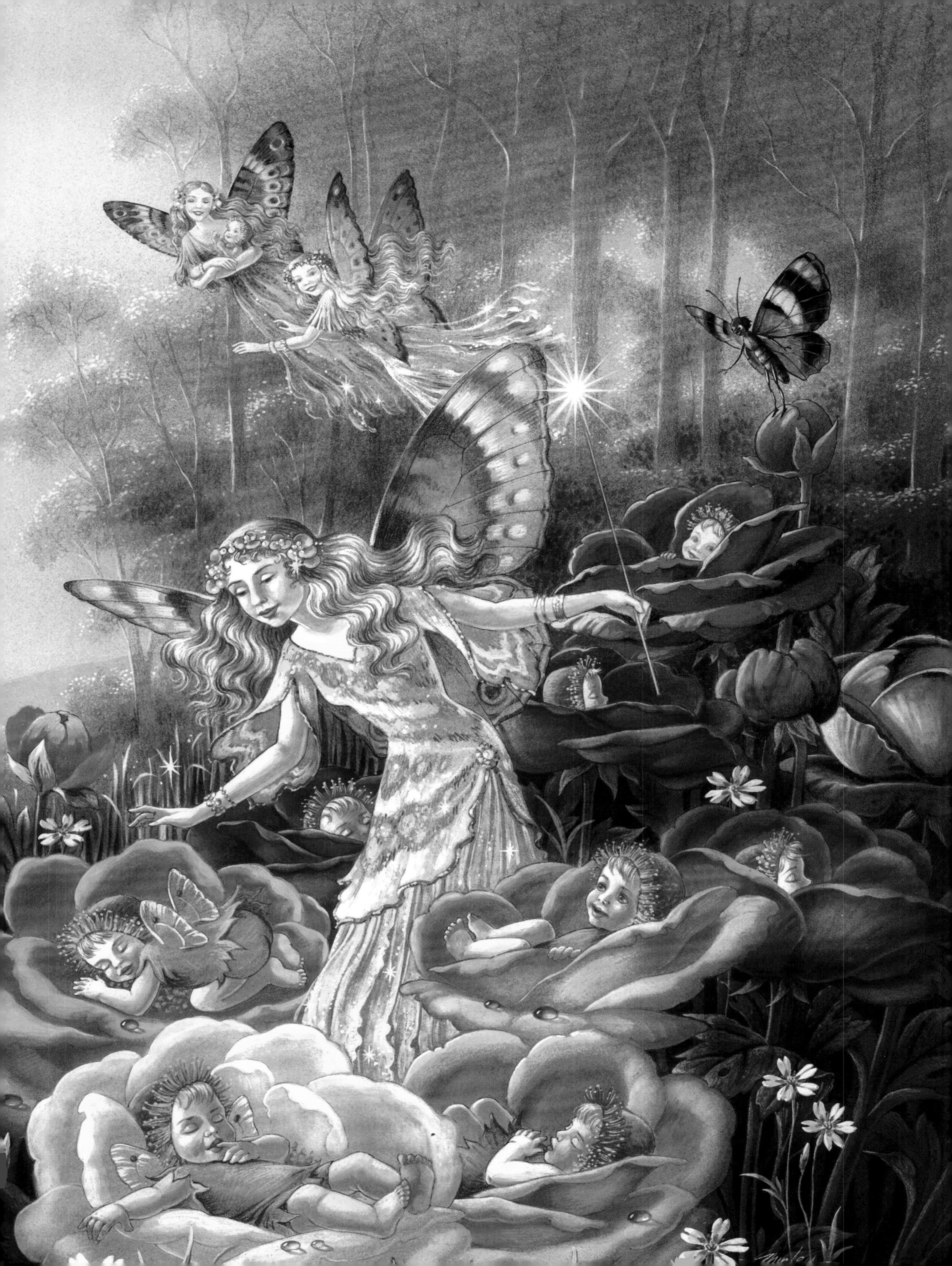

The flower nursery was bathed in warm golden light and soon the children were glad to go into some nearby woods where it was cool and shady.

A fern-fringed path led them to a lily pool where fairies were bathing and playing near a crystal spring. Laura and Daniel drank springwater from leaf-cups and paddled in the shallows.

Soon they felt cool enough to explore further.

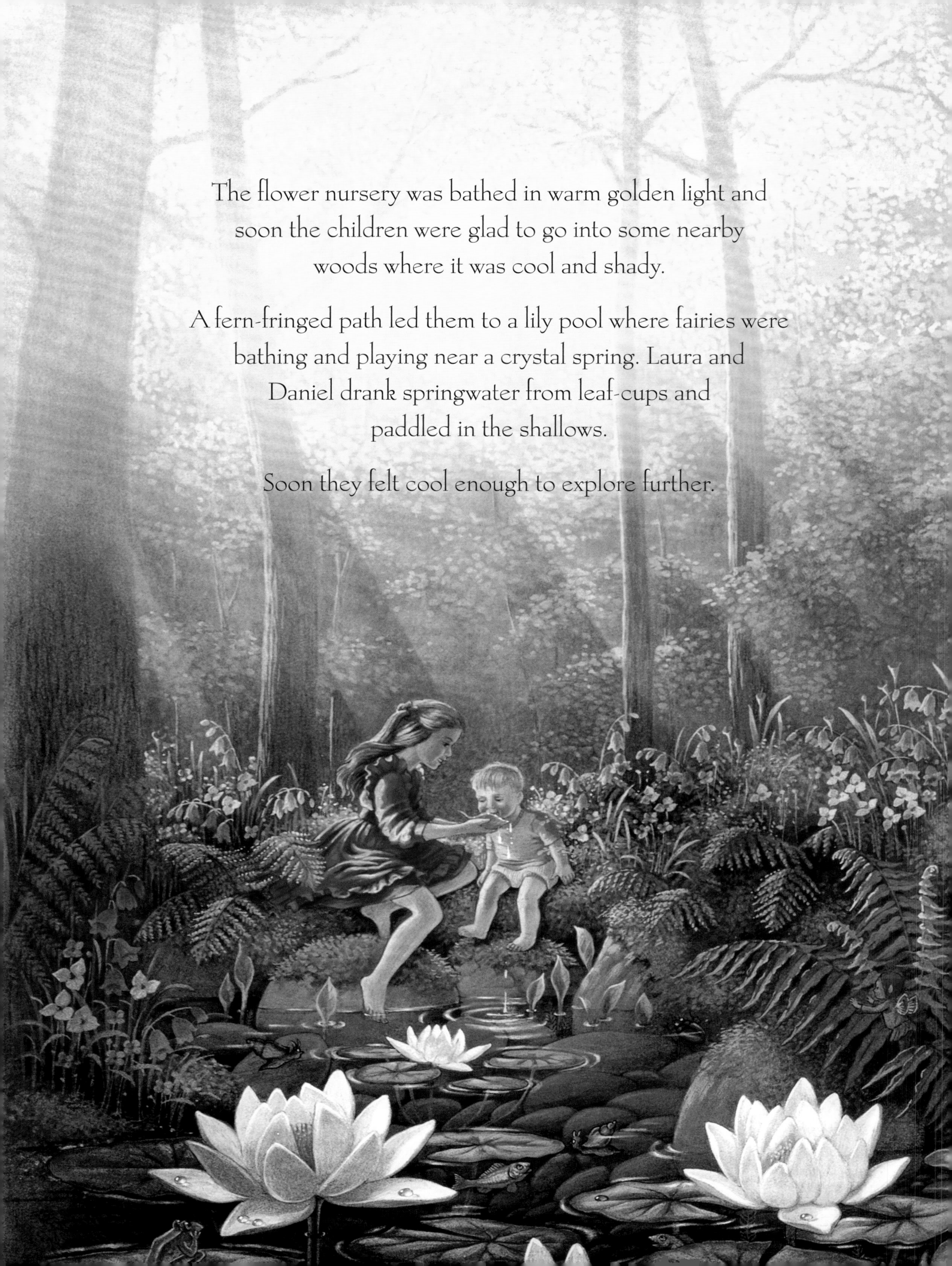

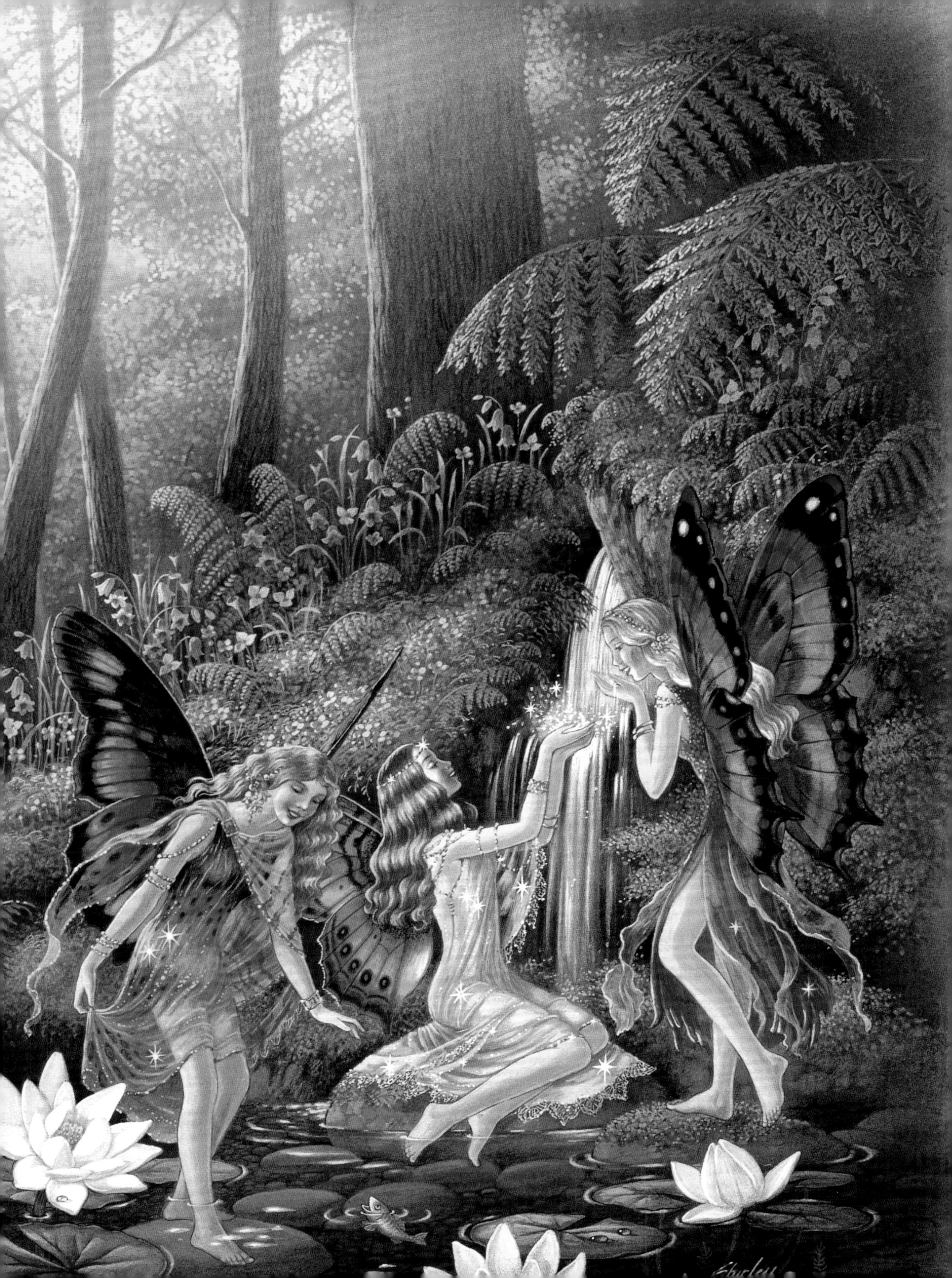

They followed the path through the woods and before long they came upon a group of elfin musicians. Rabbits, mice and frogs all had their parts to play and several fairies were dancing to the music.

"There is a ball tonight," the fairies told them, "so we are practising our steps!"

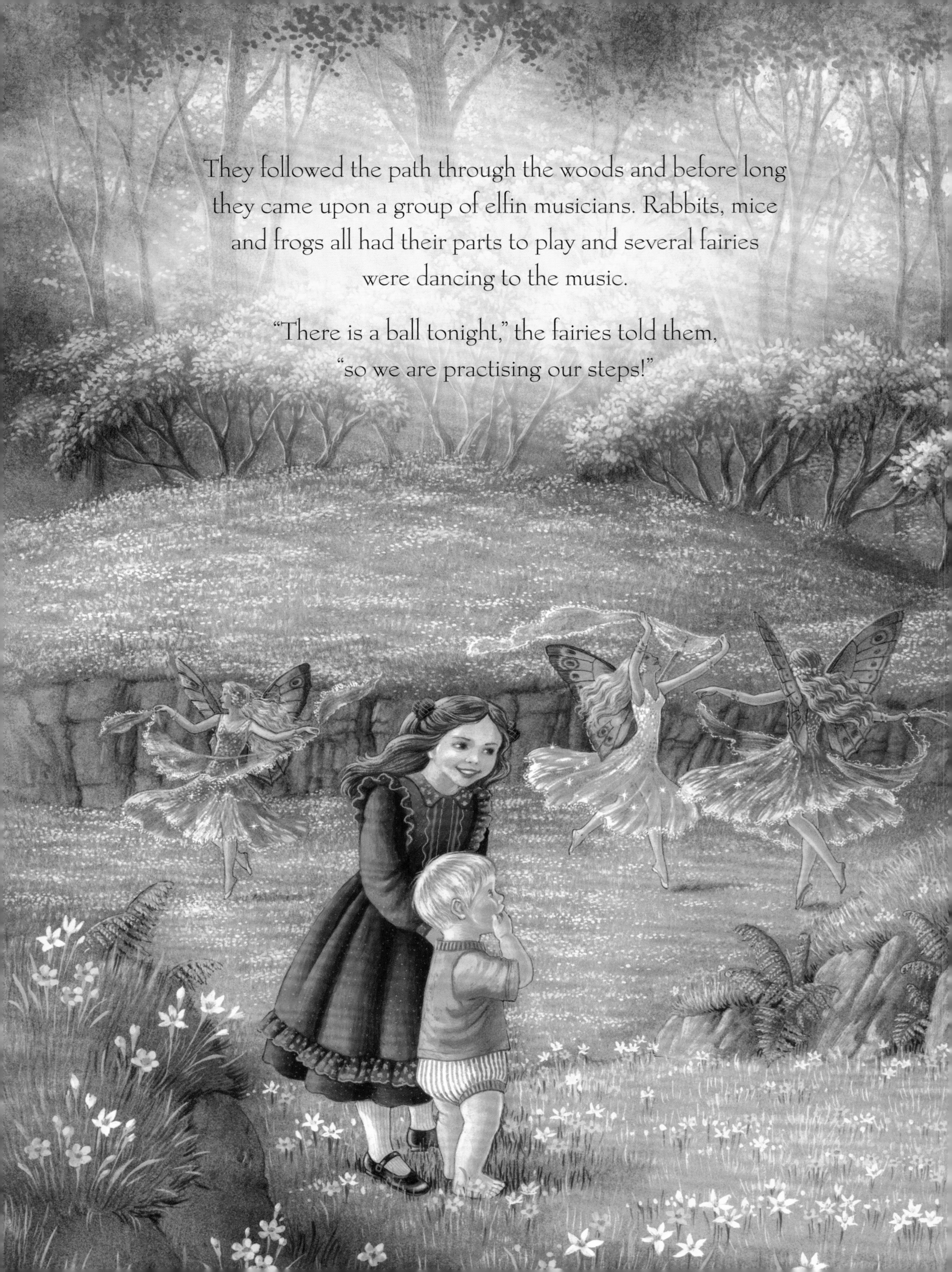

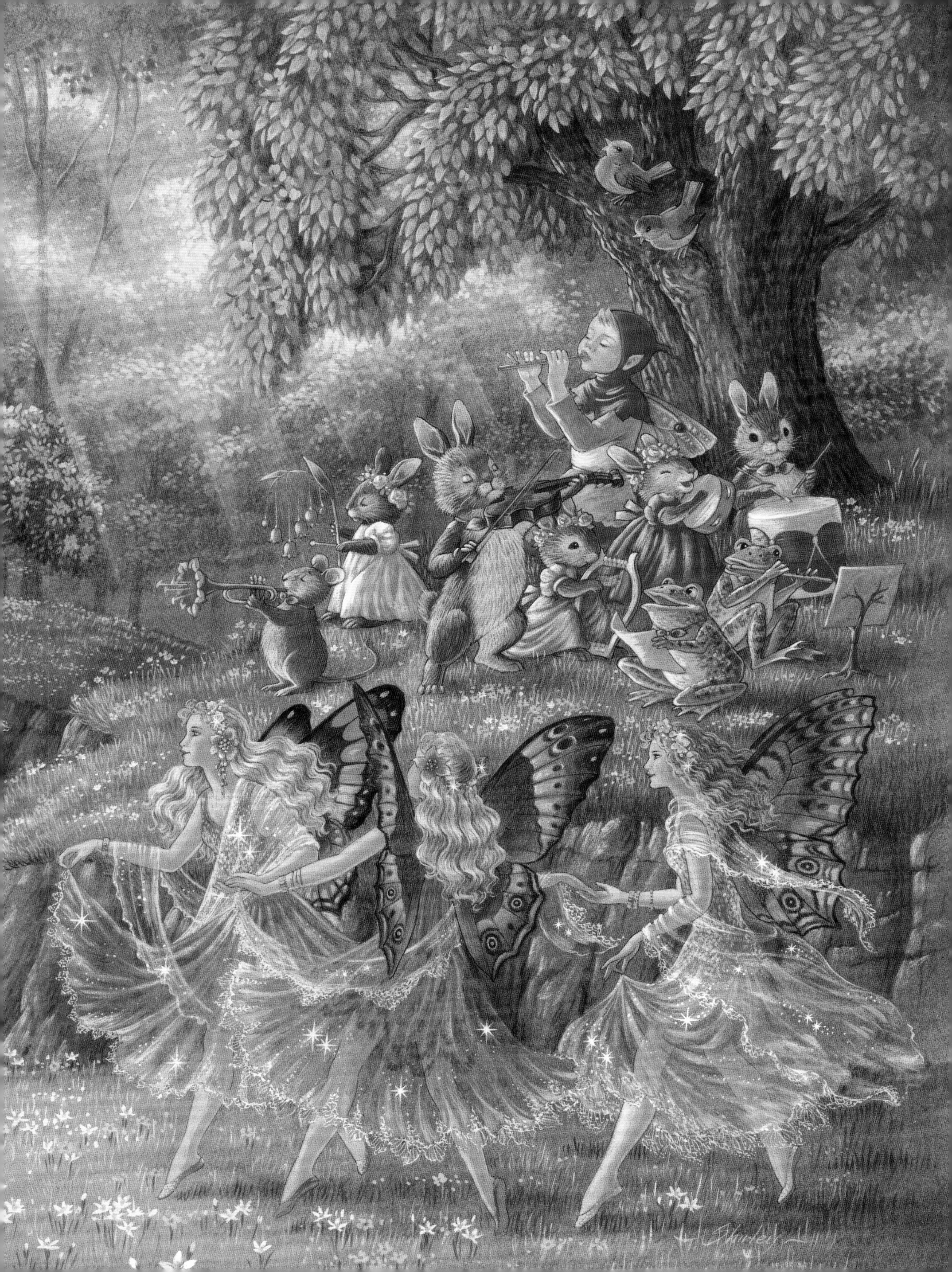

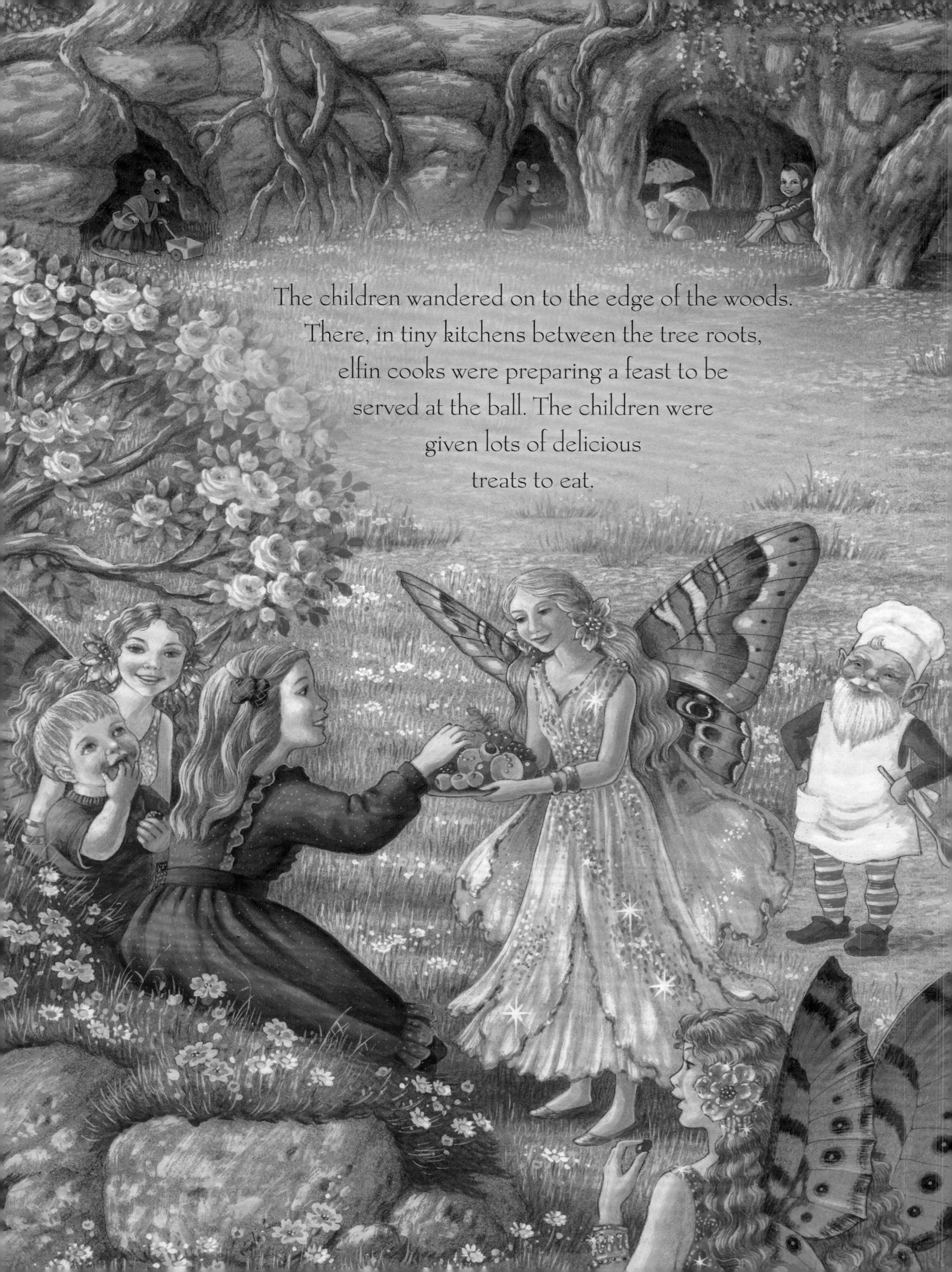

The children wandered on to the edge of the woods. There, in tiny kitchens between the tree roots, elfin cooks were preparing a feast to be served at the ball. The children were given lots of delicious treats to eat.

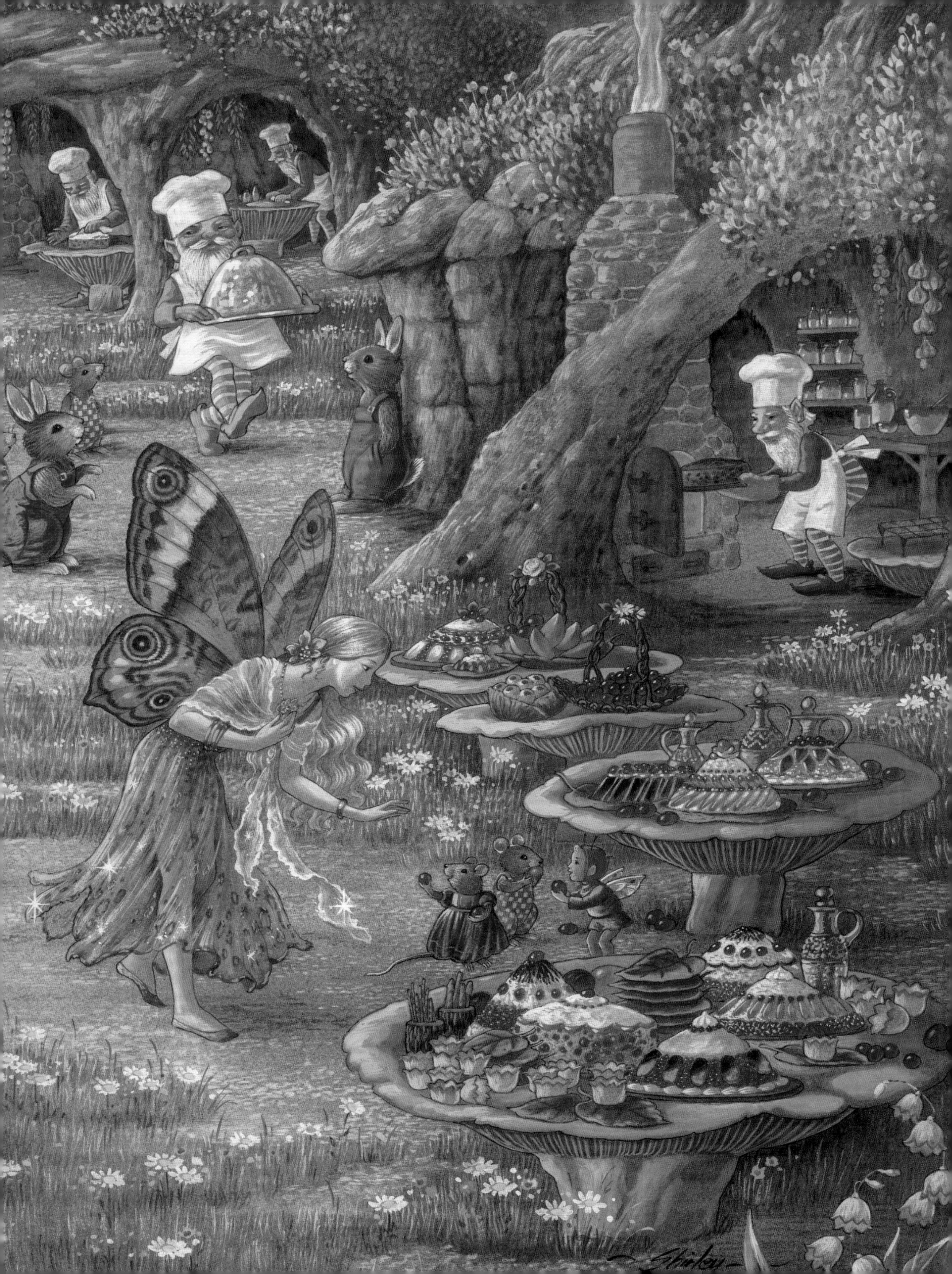

Laura talked to the fairies and elves about life in Fairyland.

"Do you ever have to do any work?" she asked.

"Oh, yes," one silver-haired fairy replied. "My work is to go out
and put frost crystals everywhere."

"Why do you do that?" Laura asked, puzzled.

"Well, when the world has been dull and gloomy and you wake to
a day where every twig and grass blade sparkles, it's suddenly
a beautiful surprise, isn't it?"

"Oh, yes it is," cried Laura. "Thank you, Silver Fairy, for all
your lovely frosty mornings!"

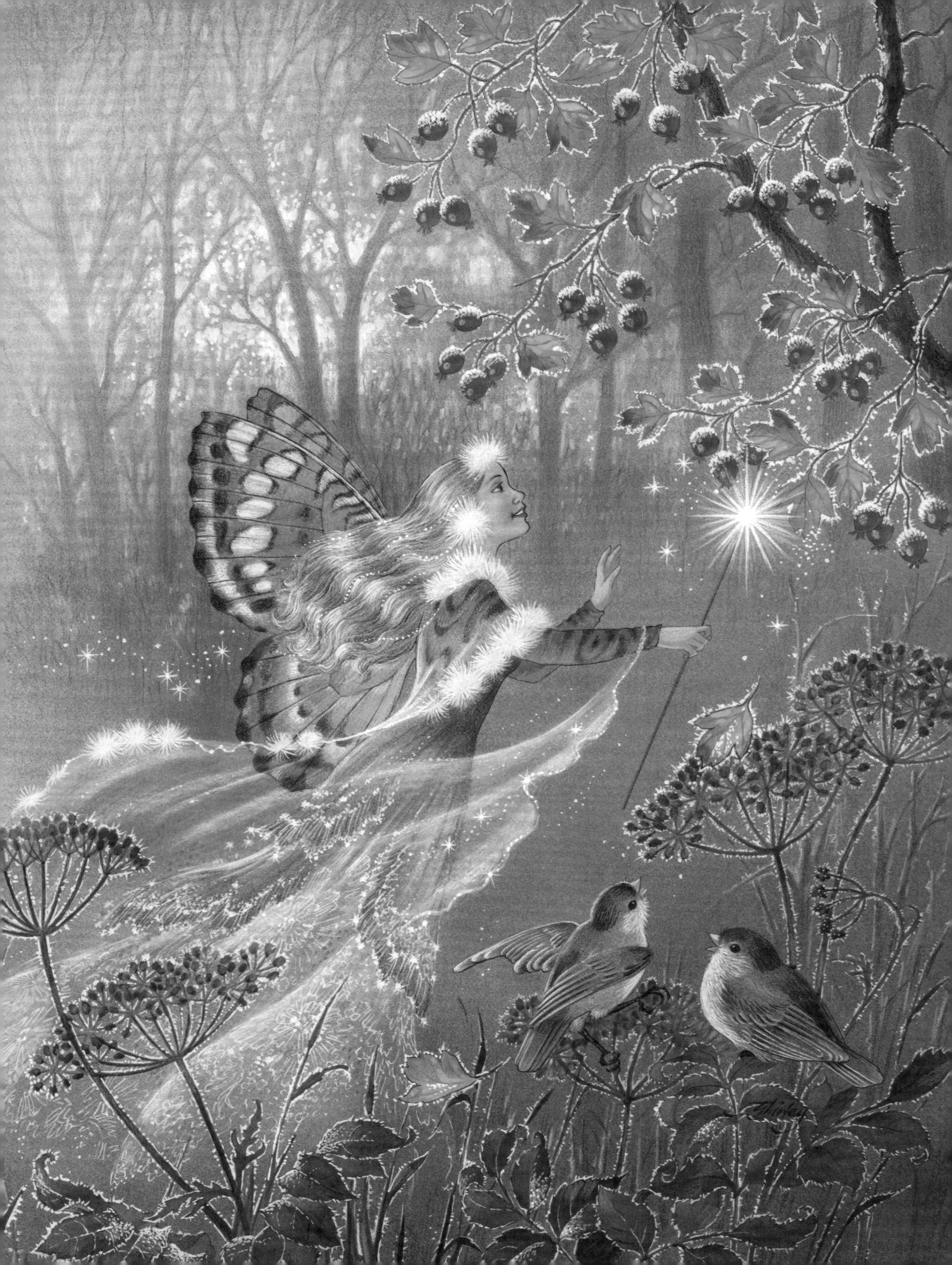

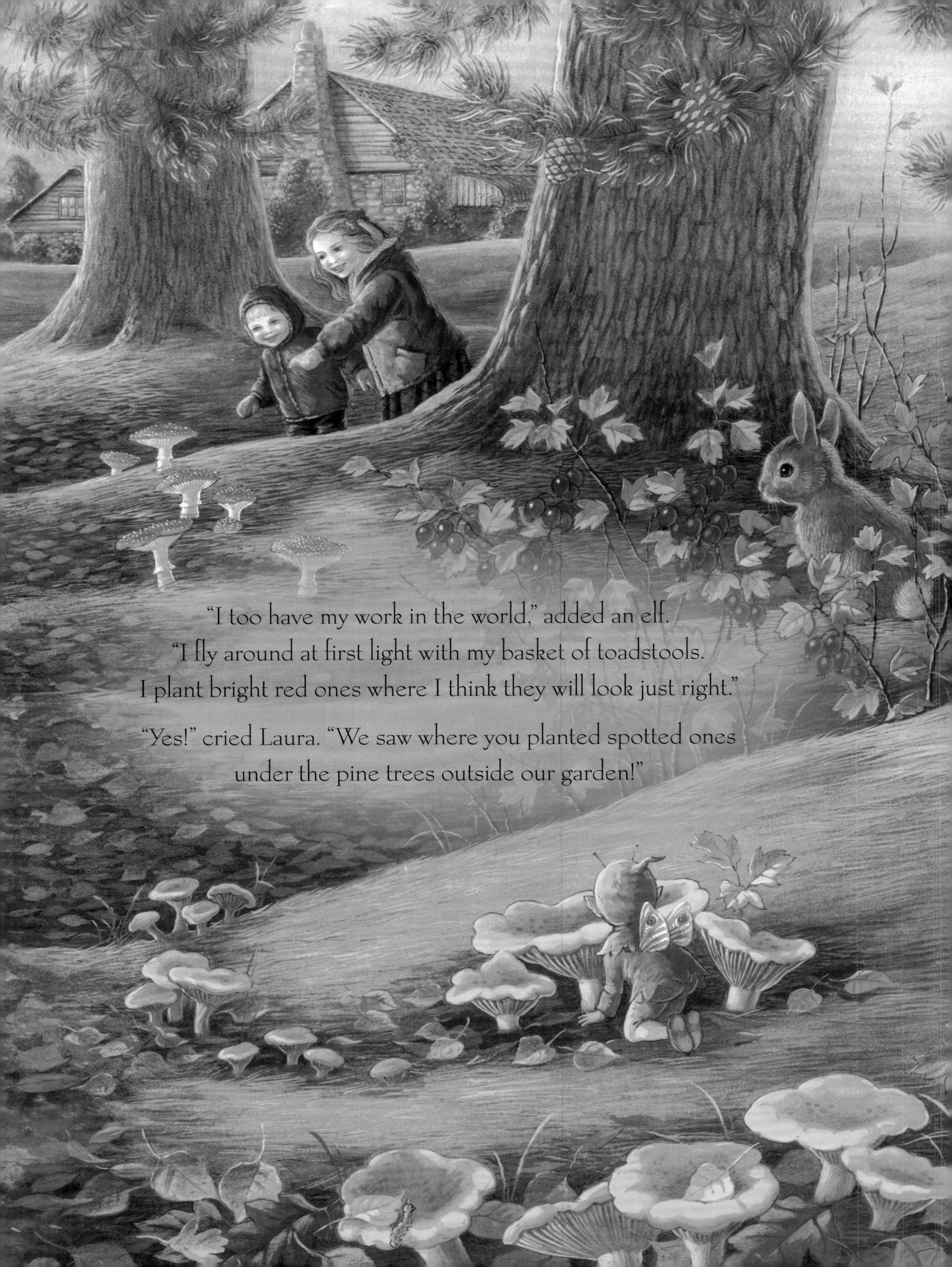

"I too have my work in the world," added an elf.
"I fly around at first light with my basket of toadstools.
I plant bright red ones where I think they will look just right."

"Yes!" cried Laura. "We saw where you planted spotted ones
under the pine trees outside our garden!"

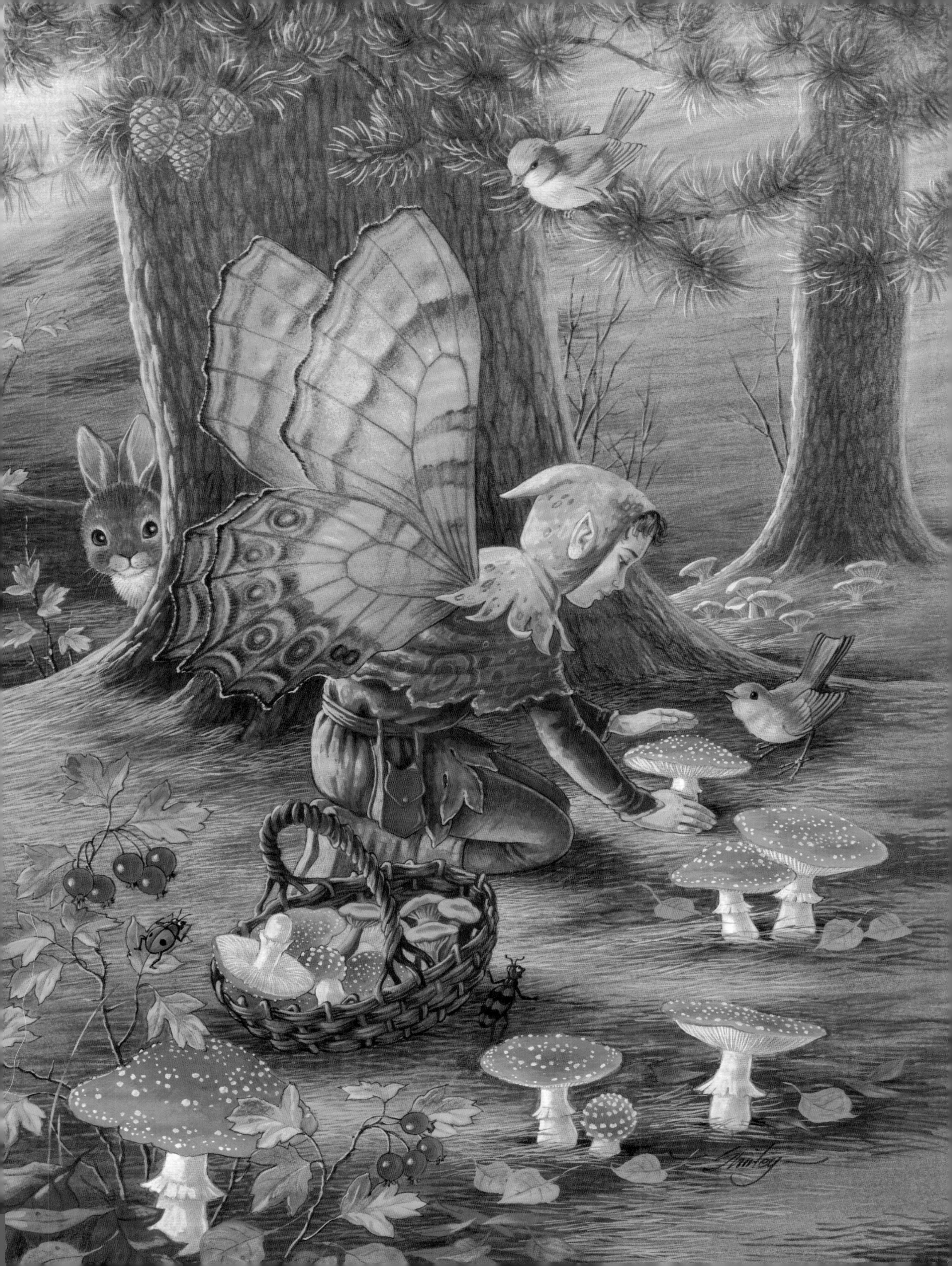

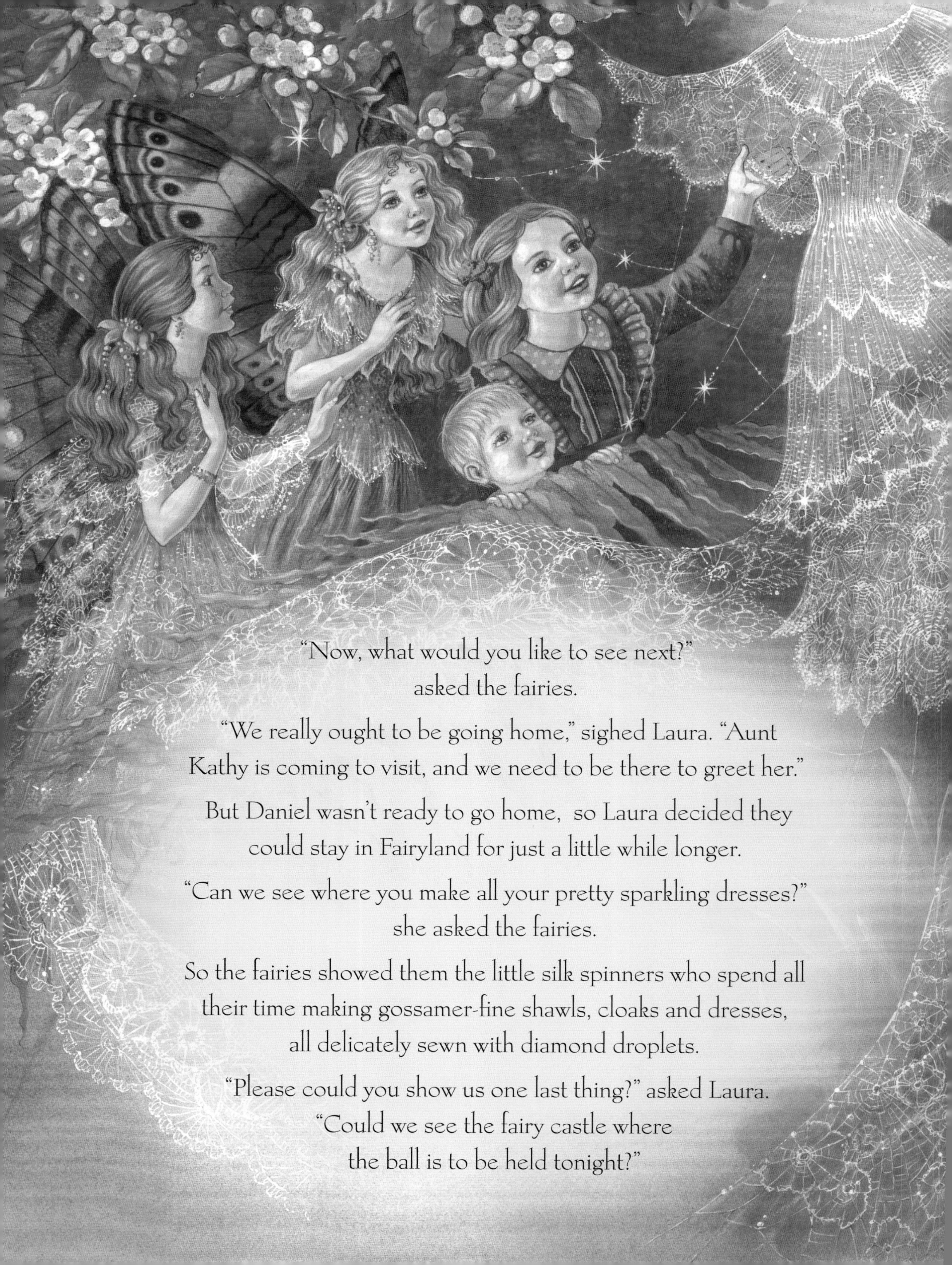

"Now, what would you like to see next?"
asked the fairies.

"We really ought to be going home," sighed Laura. "Aunt Kathy is coming to visit, and we need to be there to greet her."

But Daniel wasn't ready to go home, so Laura decided they could stay in Fairyland for just a little while longer.

"Can we see where you make all your pretty sparkling dresses?" she asked the fairies.

So the fairies showed them the little silk spinners who spend all their time making gossamer-fine shawls, cloaks and dresses, all delicately sewn with diamond droplets.

"Please could you show us one last thing?" asked Laura. "Could we see the fairy castle where the ball is to be held tonight?"

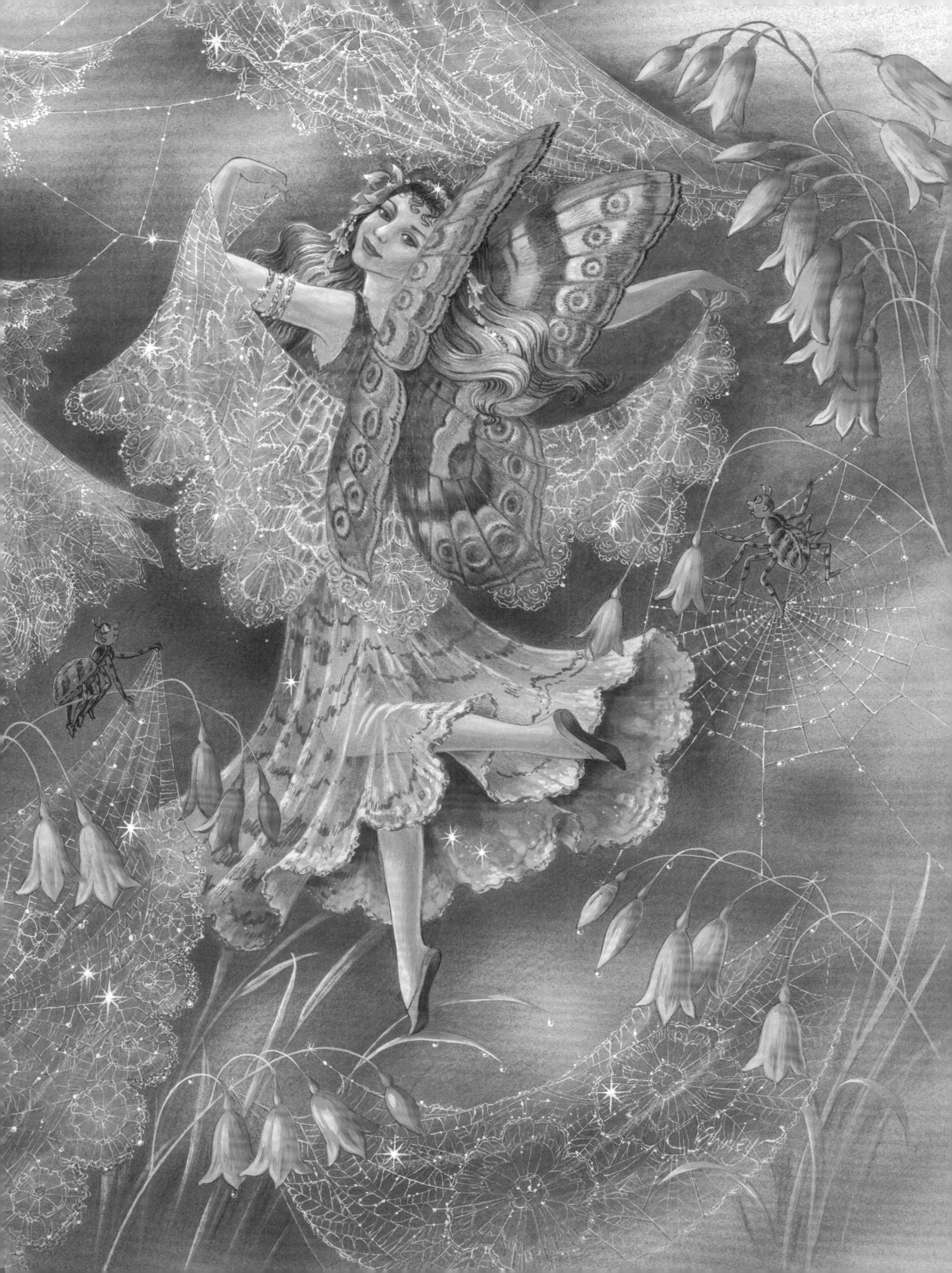

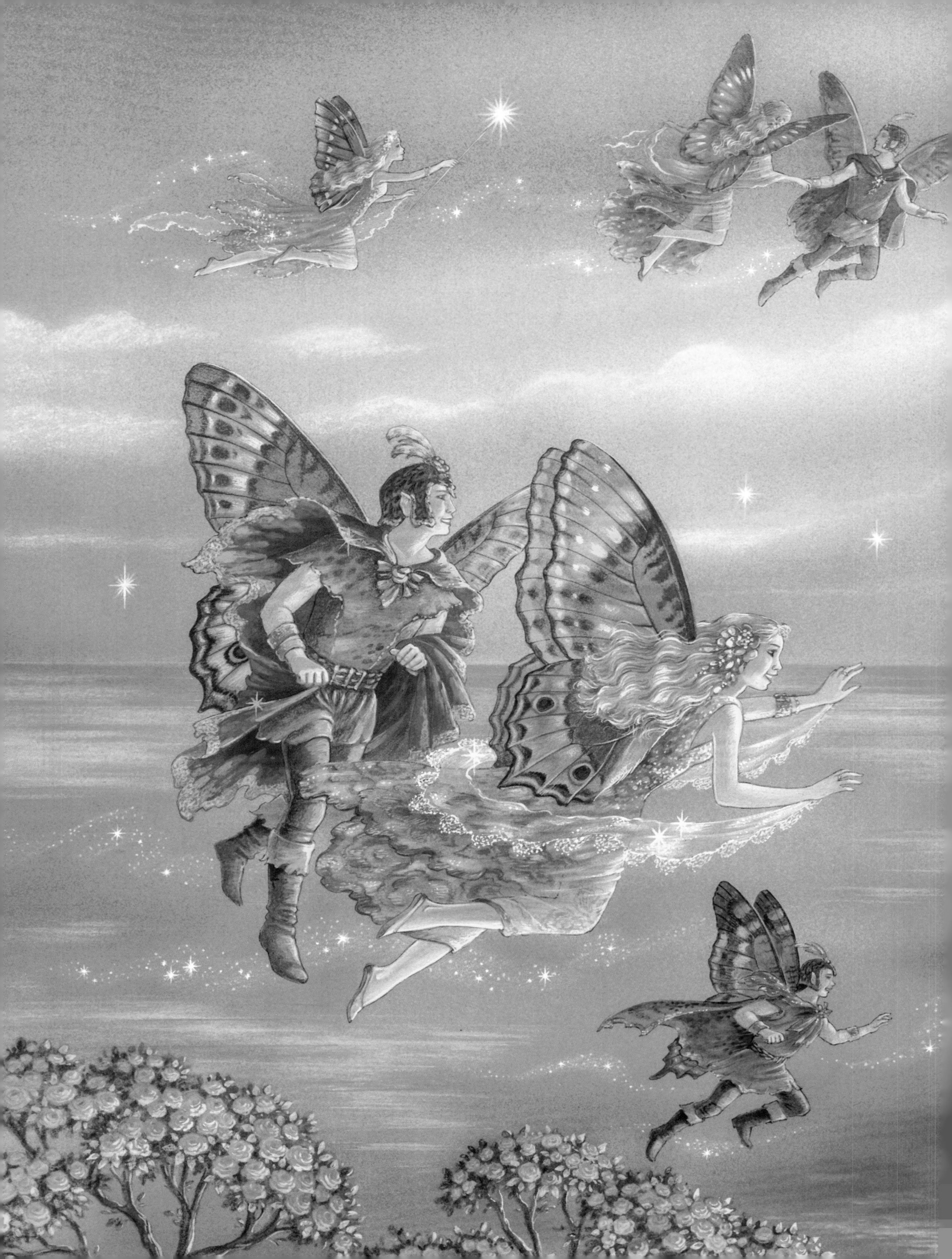

So the fairies took the children by the hand and flew them to where the fairy castle stood upon a rocky pinnacle in the sea. It shimmered in the light as fairies dressed in all their finery began to arrive for the ball.

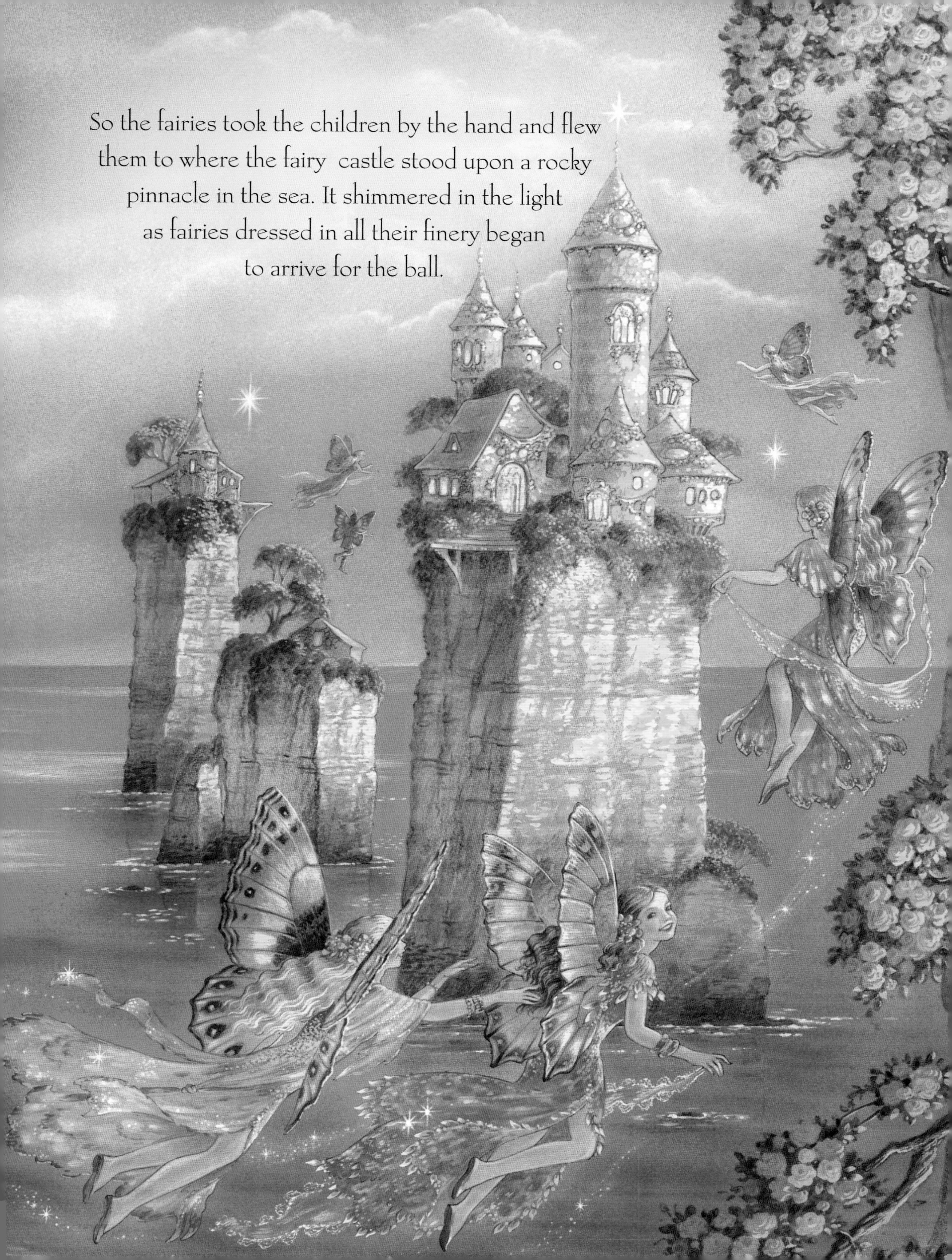

Then the fairies flew the children back to the little green door in the old willow tree. It was time for them to go home. Daniel was too tired to protest as Laura helped him crawl back through the little green doorway.

"Goodbye, Laura and Daniel," called the fairies. "Be good and kind, and you will see us again soon." Then the little green door shut and seemed to fade away.

"Come along, Danny," said Laura. "Let's go and tell our mother and Aunt Kathy all about our visit to Fairyland!"

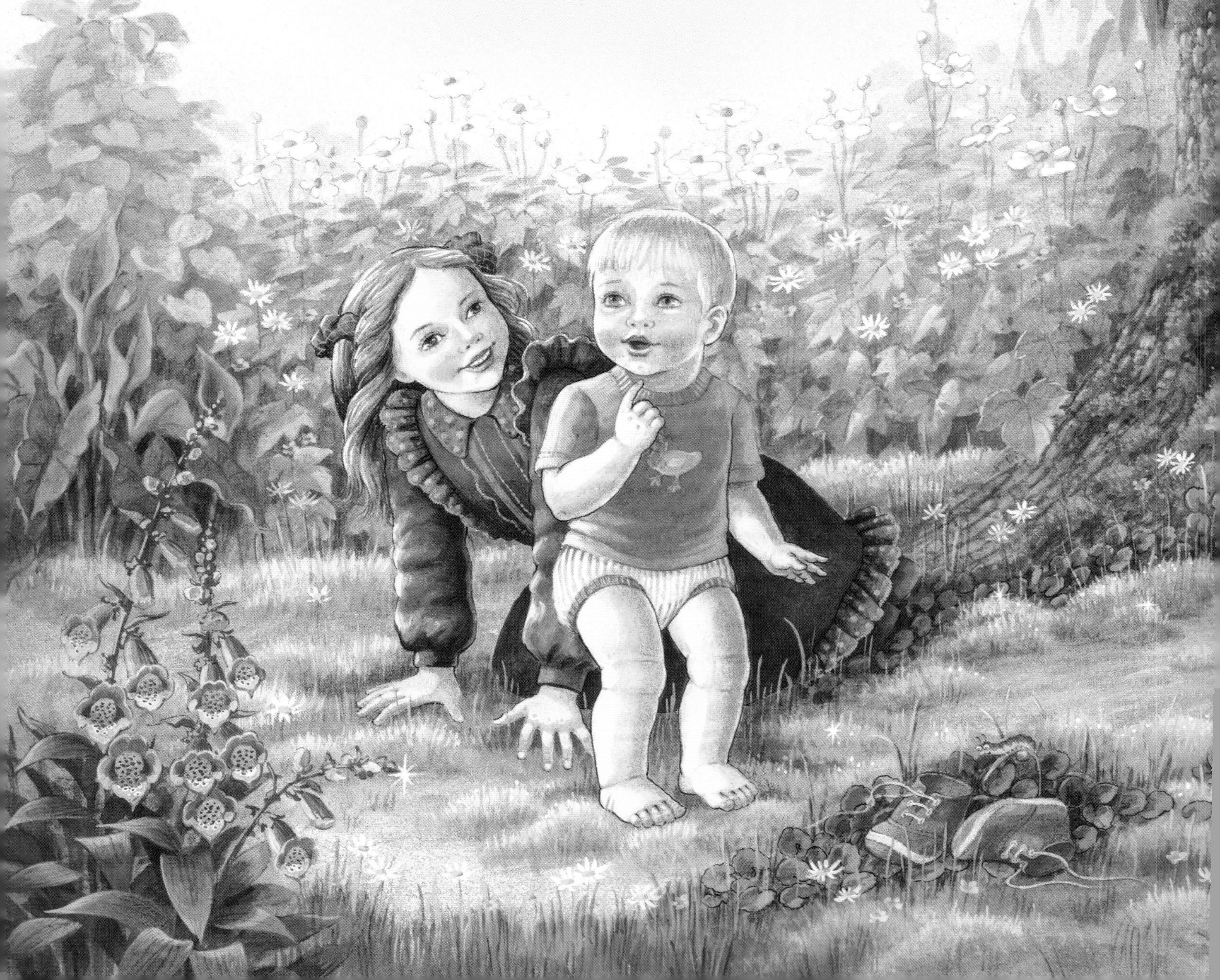

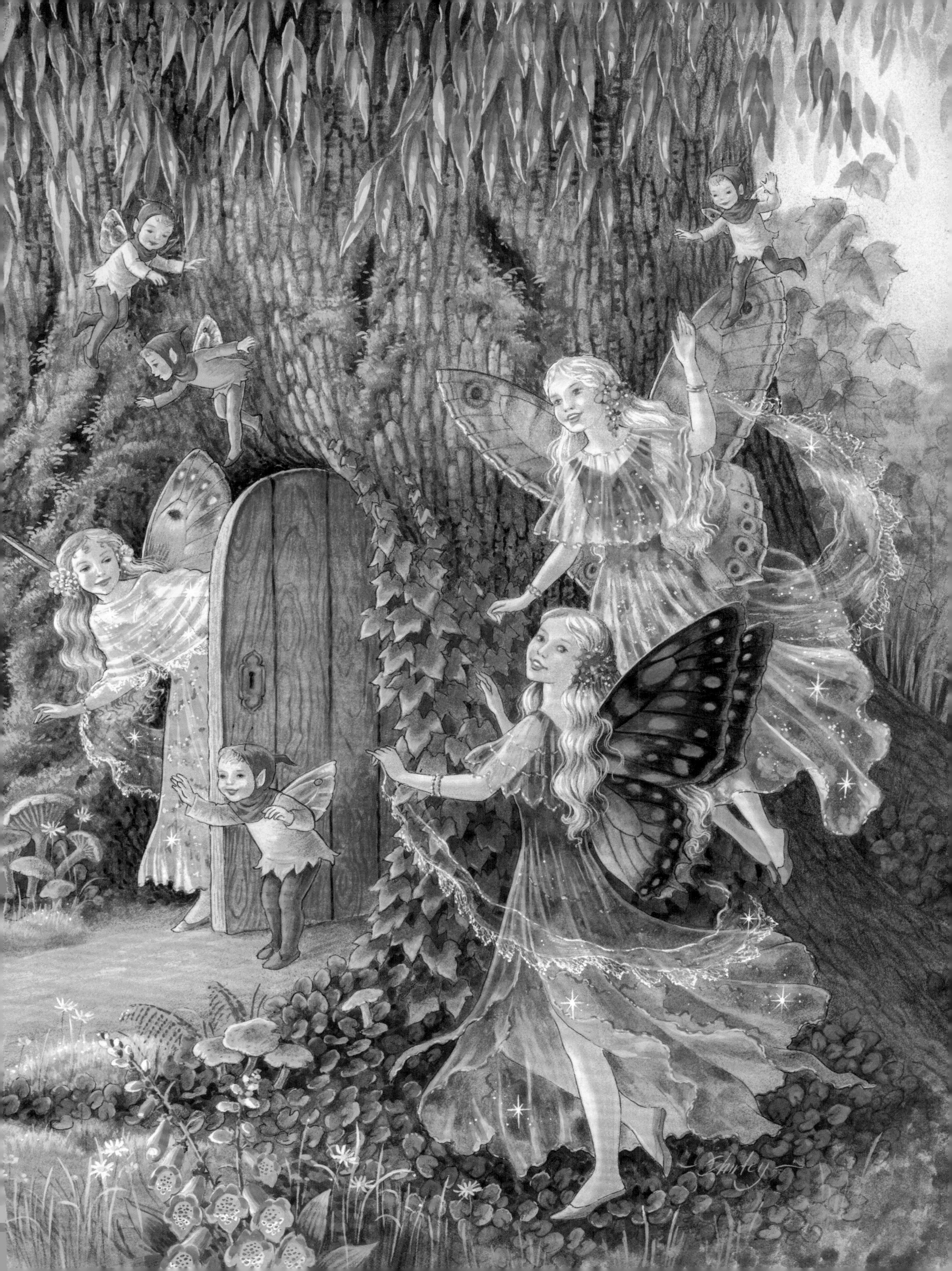
Shirley

The children found their mother laying the table for lunch. Their Aunt Kathy had arrived, and she hugged the children and gave each of them a drawing book and a packet of pencils.

"Danny's very good at drawing," Laura told her. "He can draw a box, a ball and a happy face. Danny, draw something for Aunt Kathy."

So Daniel drew a picture. But everyone was very surprised when he didn't draw a box or a ball or a happy face—he drew a fairy instead!

Published by Brolly Books, an imprint of Borghesi & Adam Publishers Pty Ltd
www.brollybooks.com email: emma@brollybooks.com. This edition first published 2019. Copyright text and illustrations ©Marbit, 2015.
Text and illustrations by Shirley Barber. Copyright design ©Brolly Books, 2019 All rights reserved. Printed in China.
Pre-Publication data is available through the National Library of Australia
ISBN 9780648457121 lenticular edition; ISBN 9780994263483 hardback